P9-DTF-900

J PB
Schubert, Leda.
Here comes Darrell
Boston : Houghton Mifflin
Co., 2005.

Discarded by
Santa Maria Library

09
11

GAYLORD MG

Here Comes Darrell

In memory of Darrell K. Farnham, 1936–2002

*To Bob, and with immense gratitude
to Mary Azarian and Ann Rider*
—L.S.

*In memory of master carpenter Luke Hardy,
my "Darrell"*
—M.A.

Text copyright © 2005 by Leda Schubert
Illustrations copyright © 2005 by Mary Azarian

All rights reserved. For information about permission to reproduce
selections from this book, write to Permissions, Houghton Mifflin
Company, 215 Park Avenue South, New York, New York 10003.

www.houghtonmifflinbooks.com

The text of this book is set in Dante MT.
The illustrations are woodcuts, hand-tinted with watercolors.

Library of Congress Cataloging-in-Publication Data
Schubert, Leda.
Here Comes Darrell / by Leda Schubert; illustrated by Mary Azarian.
p. cm.
Summary: Throughout the seasons in northern Vermont, Darrell helps his neighbors with
snowplowing, supplying wood, and excavation work, never finding time to fix his own barn,
but when a windstorm passes through town, he finds his kindness to his neighbors returned.
[1. Neighborliness—Fiction. 2. Seasons—Fiction. 3. Vermont—Fiction.] I. Azarian, Mary, ill.
II. Title. ISBN 0-618-41605-6
PZ7.S38345DAR2005 [E]—dc22 200400972 ISBN-13: 978-0-618-41605-9
WOZ 10 9 8 7 6 5 4 3 2 1

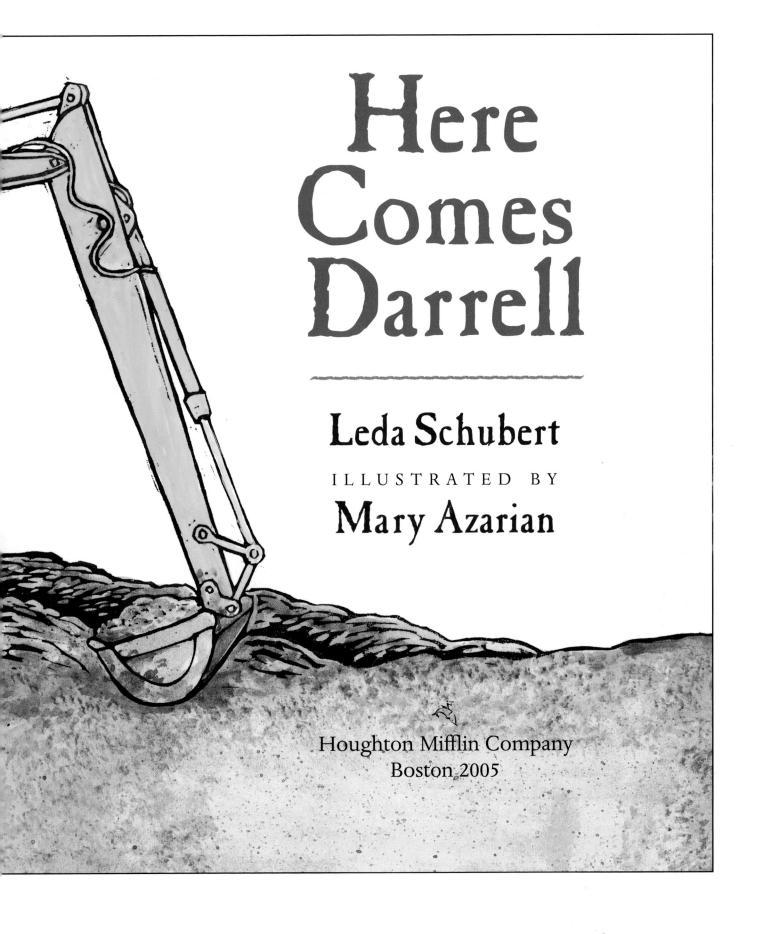

Here Comes Darrell

Leda Schubert

ILLUSTRATED BY
Mary Azarian

Houghton Mifflin Company
Boston 2005

The thermometer reads two below zero and it's snowing hard at four a.m., but Darrell is ready to work.

"I'll be home for breakfast," he says to Judy.
"I'll make eggs and home fries," she promises.

The main roads will be cleared by the town snowplows, but people with long driveways will be trapped without Darrell. His old truck starts on the second try and Buster jumps into the front seat. It's so cold that Darrell's nose hairs freeze. As he pulls away, he notices his barn roof sagging under the weight of the snow.

First Darrell plows out folks who must get to work early. Porch lights flash in thanks, and he blinks his headlights back. His stomach growls as he glimpses a neighbor making breakfast.

By seven a.m. he has plowed twenty-one driveways.

The truck radio blares, "All local schools are closed."

"Good thing. Right, Buster?" Buster barks. The roads are too slippery for schoolbuses.

The Harts' driveway is so steep and narrow that there's not much room to dump the heavy snow. As Darrell lowers the plow, the rear wheels slide off the road. He rocks the truck back and forth, back and forth. The tires swirl, the engine whines, and the back end swings closer to a ditch.

"Come on, come on." Darrell thumps the dashboard . . .

. . . and the truck jumps forward. Buster almost falls off the seat.

At the house, Tommy Hart waves. "Mom says come have coffee."

"Tell her thanks, but I've got lots more driveways."

"Can I help?"

"For a minute." Tommy climbs onto Darrell's lap and they plow a hill of snow.

"Oh boy! Mom and I can go sledding!" Tommy jumps down.

"She'll like that." Darrell says. He turns toward his twenty-third driveway and begins to think about Judy's fried eggs.

It's forty degrees when Darrell finishes loading his dump truck on a spring morning. Winter weather hangs on forever in northern Vermont, and the air still smells like wood smoke.

Since dawn Darrell has been splitting logs. The Barretts had run out of firewood and called him in a panic.

"We don't know when we'll be able to pay you," said Mr. Barrett.

"That's okay," Darrell said. "Keep those kids warm."

Just before Darrell leaves, Judy calls, "Don't forget about our barn roof.
Looks like a good wind will lift it right off."

Darrell picks up Buster. "I'll get to it soon," he says.

Mud season has arrived, and the dirt roads are like chocolate pudding. The truck hits a rut and shoots sideways, sinking into a hole at the bottom of the Barretts' hill. Darrell and Buster wade through the mud up to the house.

"Looks like I'm stuck," he tells them.

"We're coming," says Mrs. Barrett. The Barretts and their two kids, David and Beth, help Darrell unload the wood.

"I'll be back for the truck," Darrell says. That evening, when the ruts freeze, Judy will bring him over on the tractor and they'll pull the truck out.

"We'll drive you home," Mrs. Barrett offers. "But come in first for some apple pie."

"No time. But I almost forgot these." He hands carefully carved birds to David and Beth.

"Will you teach me to whittle?" Beth asks.

"Sure." When his own kids were little, Darrell taught them to whittle, too.

Beth grins. "Then I'm going to learn to carve a dog just like Buster."

It's eighty-five degrees and the black flies are biting when Darrell starts his backhoe. The Murphys are building a new room, and Darrell is the excavator.

Judy reminds him about the barn. "Winter will be here sooner than we think."

"It doesn't look that bad," Darrell says, but it does.

The backhoe is a large machine, but Darrell is an artist. If a hammer drops on the ground, he can pick it up with the big bucket as if he's using tweezers.

He begins scooping and moves load after load of earth.

The Murphys arrive as he finishes digging. Andy Murphy throws a ball for Buster and it flies into the hole. Buster jumps in after it and can't climb out. "Sorry!" Andy cries.

"Don't worry, Andy." Darrell swings the bucket around, gently picks up Buster, and deposits him on the bank. Buster shakes off.

"You folks interested in a pond over there?" Darrell asks. He points down the hill. "It'll be great for frogs and birds."

"I want frogs," Andy says, and his parents nod yes.

The Murphys hear the backhoe for the rest of the day, and the next, and the next. Every day Andy brings his frog net and watches the pond fill with water.

It's fifty degrees and the wind is fierce when Darrell, Judy, and Buster climb into the old truck on a brilliant October day. They are off to visit neighbors to see what everybody needs before winter. Judy keeps a list.

"What about our barn?" she asks.

"Tomorrow. I promise," Darrell says. And he means it, because soon the cows will have to come inside.

Some people need to have their driveways fixed. Some need firewood.
The wind picks up and the list grows longer. Tree branches crash onto
the road, and Darrell holds tight to the steering wheel on a gusty hill.

"Now *I'm* worried about that roof," he says.

When they get home, their barn roof is gone.

Darrell slams on the brakes and jumps out of the truck. Buster runs in wild circles. They hurry to the barn, where the Harts and Barretts are already taking measurements.

Mr. Murphy greets Darrell. "We saw it go and rushed right over," he explains.

"We're going to have a roof raising!" says Beth Barrett.

Darrell looks so embarrassed that Mr. Murphy says, "You've helped all of us over and over. We're happy to help you."

Mrs. Hart leads Darrell to the table. "We brought over some supper. Come and eat."

It is getting dark outside, but inside it feels as if the sun is shining. Beth Barrett, Andy Murphy, and Tommy Hart bring Darrell and Judy heaping plates of stew and pie, and everybody is safe and sound, even Darrell.